THEIR FRUITS LIKE HONEY

A SAPPHIC FAE RETELLING ROMANCE

GODSTOUCHED UNIVERSE

ALI WILLIAMS

This one's for Ash, for tarot, art and friendship.

AUTHOR NOTE

Please be aware that this story contains references to death (off-page, centuries before the story), consensual non-consent (on page, more "force me" energy than anything else, fully consensual and longed for), and kink (lots of it!). I hope I have treated Lizzie and Aoibheall's experiences and emotions with the care that they and you deserve.

1

Lizzie

I am not one for sex clubs.

I'm not really one for anything other than cosy cardigans, perfect book nooks, and the stacks in the library where I work.

Genuinely, the last thing that I want to do is to come to the infamous Golden Apple club. And yet here I am.

I straighten my glasses, somewhat awkwardly, and shuffle on the spot. Standing here for the last half an hour, building up the courage to walk in, I've seen some of the most beautiful people walk through the club's doors. Tall and willowy, with striking hair and eyes that seem like they'd be able to see into your soul.

My hair is brown. Mousy brown. I'm short and fat, and I'm the furthest thing from remarkable that you could possibly imagine. Living my life in the shadows is exactly what I want from it, nothing more, nothing less. Books and shadows and no one looking too hard at me.

But even unremarkable people have their limit.

Laura's been missing for hours. *Hours.* And I know that she applied and got accepted to this club, and so this is where I am, ready to storm the doors and take down any depraved individual who may have kidnapped my sister.

Admittedly, it's highly likely that Laura just didn't want to leave, but I'm not taking that risk, she can be pissed off with me. It's better than finding her body floating in a river somewhere.

I really should stop reading quite so many crime novels. I'm sure real life isn't anywhere near as interesting as all that.

Steeling myself, I clench my hands into tight fists and stride towards the club door. The golden apple flashes neon as I pull the door open and walk in. No knocking and waiting for me, because if I wait a moment longer, I know I'll lose my nerve and leave.

The reception is not the least what I expect. It's well-lit, and the person behind the desk is dressed chicly, as if they're working for some well-paying business firm in one of the big cities.

"You didn't knock," they say, and I muster every ounce of courage that I have to reply.

"I did not. I need to see my sister."

They look me up and down, a slow movement that has their eyes dragging over my outfit. "Not without membership, and not dressed like that."

I glance down at my sensible shoes, sensible skirt and sensible blouse, adjust the glasses primly on my nose, and try not to feel like an eighty-year-old spinster. "Try and stop me." I'm the least threatening figure in the world, I know that, but I'm also stubborn. Stubbornness has gotten me this far and it'll get me inside the main club as well.

They stand up, and in an instant I feel a flash of fear, like they're some predator sizing up prey. But they haven't had to handle a group of bored teenagers on a Friday afternoon when there's nowhere else for them to go but the library. I've had boys fronting off to me, and I've also had them back all the way down the moment I raised an eyebrow.

This person may be dressed better than me, they may have more experience of the world than me, but there is nothing that they can do to keep me from my sister. I won't allow it.

We stand, looking at each other, neither gaze faltering.

"Why are you here?" they offer eventually, once they realise that I'm not going to back down.

"To see my sister," I say. "She's been missing for twenty-four hours and I'm not going anywhere until I know that she's okay."

They mutter something under their breath that sounds remarkably like fucáil, and I say "Mind your language," without even thinking about it. The look they shoot me is full of loathing and I'm fairly certain that they want to say something a fair bit stronger, but bite their tongue instead.

"How about we fetch her out?"

"No. I'm going in to see her."

"It's more than my job's worth to let you do that."

"Then I guess I'll speak to your manager about the situation." I'm sounding like every jumped-up overly-protective woman in the village who insists on speaking to my boss instead of me at the library about the content of our books. I sound like a Karen—for want of a better word—and I hate it. But it's the only thing that's keeping this mask affixed to my face, and I'm clinging to it with everything that I've got.

Follow the rules.

That was drilled into me, by my family, by my teachers, by society. If you follow the rules, the outcome is clear—at least, that's the lie neurotypicals tell themselves. But if I borrow this façade and pretend that I am normal, that I know the rules, if I don't bend... then maybe, just maybe, I'll get what I want in this scenario.

When I get home, I'll curl up in a ball and cry, most likely. I don't like talking to strangers out of the context of work. At least there I know the rules. Here it's like walking a tightrope whilst it shakes over and over and I struggle to remain upright.

A light flickers behind me and I flinch. I prefer it when lights remain steady, otherwise it feels uncomfortable, like there's actual pain in my head, pressure building behind my eyeballs.

I make the slightest of adjustments to my stance so that the flickering moves out of my eyeline, and sigh in relief.

My nemesis behind the desk picks up a phone and mutters into it in low, hushed tones. Then they hang up and look back at me. "Aoibheall is coming."

"Excellent," I say, not having the faintest idea who that is, and take a seat opposite the reception desk.

I don't have to wait long. The main doors swing open and shut behind the most dramatic looking woman I've ever seen.

"Naoise, where is this mortal who dares take up my time?" Her words are as icy as she is hot, and I don't mean that aesthetically, I mean it literally. The heat rolling off this woman is overwhelming, like stepping into a sauna at a spa. Sweat drips from my forehead down the side of my face and I try to focus on this woman, this Aoibheall.

She's dressed as if she's from another age entirely, with hair that moves about her as if it were an aura, surrounding her. Hair that's so blond, it's almost white, and sharp green eyes that take me in angrily as she turns.

I can't do anything but stare. All the people I've seen walk through those doors this evening—all those *beautiful* people—cannot hold even a flickering candle to her.

"Is it you?" she demands, rather than asks. Her lip curls and distaste rolls off her in waves. In any other scenario it would make me shrink, but I'm not making myself smaller, not when my sister may need me.

"That's right," I say and—going against every autistic instinct in my being—raise my eyes to meet hers. Their green is dark. I could drown in them. "I want to see my sister."

2

Aoibheall

I have no time for mortals.

They are fickle and flighty, and have no respect or loyalty beyond their own wants and needs.

My instinct is to dismiss this woman out of hand, but there's something in her dark eyes that stops me. She's meeting my gaze, holding it for far longer than most immortals would, and yet there's an unsurety in the way she stands, shifting from foot to foot, as if even this much eye contact discomforts her.

"Why are you moving like that?" I ask.

She blinks and looks away, and I feel a rush of satisfaction that I have irritated her. "I'm autistic," she says, biting out the words as if having to explain herself is painful. "I don't like making eye contact." And then she raises her head and stares right at me again.

I'm impressed, despite myself, and curious too. What is it that drives her to do something that she so clearly dislikes? "You are a strange thing," I say.

She bristles. "Well, that's just downright rude. I'd ask for an apology if I thought you had any idea what that was." She blinks slowly, never moving her gaze from my face, but her fists are clenched tight.

I'm the one to break first, looking away from this tiny determined moral. "Who are you?"

"Lizzie Byrne," she says. "I believe that my sister, Laura Byrne, is a member here?"

There aren't many mortals who are members here, and of those who are, Laura Byrne doesn't ring a bell. Most of them barely leave a whisper of an impression on me. I don't play with mortals, not unless I'm feeling cruel. My sister does. Clíodhna fell in love with a mortal whose presence I tolerate, the same way I tolerate the Dark Goddess' mortal. But this Laura Byrne...

Naoise clears their throat and I look over at them. "What? Spit it out."

Their eyes widen and I realise that I *have* heard that name before. Not in its entirety, but the first name? That's the name of the girl tied up on the stage, passing in and out of consciousness.

Mortals come to our club on occasion; they join in the hopes of achieving bliss that somehow eludes them elsewhere, and we are always clear about what that may entail. This woman's sister is one such mortal, and her appetites outstripped even the most depraved of the fae. She wished to be broken, a self-destruction that I hadn't seen in such a virulent strain since we'd been freed from beyond the Veil.

Everything was consensual, everything pre-agreed, but I doubt that this bristling woman will believe that when she sees the marks on her sister's skin.

"Perhaps, Naoise, you could go and fetch Laura from her scene."

Lizzie's eyes darken and I can tell that she knows something is amiss. "What aren't you telling me?" she demands.

"Many things," I bite back. As a Queen of the Fae, I'm not used to being addressed in such a manner. But it's more than that. I dislike people at the best of times, but this Lizzie is riling me like no one else.

"There's no need to be snarky," she says, and gives a little angry wriggle. It's a slight movement, a shifting of her hips, but it's so sharp that I can feel her suppressed emotion. I want to feed on it, but I'm no leannán sídhe, drawing a mortal's life energy from them. So instead I glower in her direction and turn back to Naoise. "Did I stutter?"

Naoise is used to me, so their eyes just shutter as they get up and head towards the main club room.

Lizzie glares at me. "You can't talk to them like that. When they come back, I'll give them the number for my union, because that is unacceptable behaviour." She places her hands on her hips, and I have to fight to stop myself from snarling at her.

"What use have we for mortal unions?" My anger rises now. "You think you know anything about us, and this place; you cannot even comprehend the things you do not know." I am baiting her, I know it, challenging her to push me that little extra inch further, but at my words she pauses, looking unsure. "What now?"

"*Mortal* unions?"

Fuck.

Those few mortals who become members are told some —basic—truths. Of who we are. Of the dangers of playing with the fae. But it is never me who imparts this information. My sister, Clíodhna, bears that responsibility. And now I have allowed myself to be so goaded that I have spoken without thinking.

The doors behind us wing open then and Naoise and my sister enter, half carrying Laura between them. I have never in all my centuries been so glad to see my sister. So glad that I'm not even angry that her mortal is following them.

Lizzie turns her back on me instantly, and it feels like a dismissal, and I got say something only I catch sight of her face. She is looking at Laura—half anxiety, half anger—and when Laura lifts her head and says, "For fuck's sake Lizzie, what are you doing here? I was having fun," even I feel a wave of sympathy for her.

"I was worried, Laura. You didn't reply to any of my messages."

Her sister throws herself onto a chair and nods her thanks at Naoise and Clíodhna. "Because I was tied up. Having fun. Remember that? Fun?"

Janet steps forward. "It was all consensual, I can assure you of that."

"Of course, it fucking was," mutters Laura, and my ire transfers from one sister to the other. "I can't do anything without you checking up on me."

"Twenty-four hours," says Lizzie, and her voice is small and tight, as if she's clinging onto the words for support. "You went to a sex club you'd never been to before, and didn't check-in for twenty-four hours."

"That's perfectly normal," her sister begins, but I'm having none of that.

"It's written into your membership contract that you have to do check-ins." Everyone does, mortal or otherwise. The last thing we want are visits from concerned families or worse, the Garda. "No wonder your sister was concerned. Your membership is forfeit."

Clíodhna raises an eyebrow at my words, but she doesn't challenge my judgement.

Laura swivels on the seat, looking at each of the women —and Naoise—standing near her, and her eyes fill with tears. As if that will soften my decision. I'm not some fickle child to be swayed by such things.

"Take your sister home," I say to Lizzie and am about to turn to leave when I stop. There is something about the energy in this room that feels wrong.

The two sisters are watching each other, Lizzie warily, Laura with undisguised fury. The contrast between them both is stark, though the resemblance is still there. They look more like sister than Clíodhna and I do, though the hate that paints Laura's face is eerily familiar. I've seen it in the mirror, and I've seen it across from me, and both times I disliked how it felt.

"I'm not going anywhere with *her*," says Laura eventually, and when she stands and moves, presumably towards the cloakroom to get her things, she shoves Lizzie to the floor.

My sister is instantly behind me, arm across my throat, holding me back.

I know why.

I'd have stabbed the bitch.

There's a gentle huff of resignation behind us, and Lizzie picks herself off the floor, dusts down her clothes, and nods at us. She no longer meets my eyes.

"Deal with that one," I mutter at Clíodhna, and leave her to deal with the disloyal mortal. "I shall deal with *her*."

3

Lizzie

"**C**ome with me." Aoibheall says. I don't particularly want to go, but there's not much else that I can do in this moment. I know this mood of Laura's, and she'll be pissed at me for a good while yet.

I suppose it's partly justified, perhaps I did overreact, but she's my only family, and she had said that she'd check-in with me and I'd heard *nothing*. What was I supposed to think?

A cool grip around my wrist, makes me look up, and Aoibheall is striding towards the stairs, and I'm so short that I have to jog to keep up. "Where are we going?"

"Somewhere that disloyal bitch is not."

She's not wrong, but she doesn't get to say that. A squawk of annoyance leaves my lips, and she stops halfway up the stairs, and then looks over at where Laura is arguing with the other members of staff. "*That* is whom you're protecting." It's not a question, though there is surprise in her voice.

"She's my sister," I say firmly.

"So's Clíodhna, but I wouldn't care if someone called her a disloyal bitch if she behaved like your sister."

I yank my wrist free and glare at her. "Stop it."

"Fine." There's something akin to grudging respect in the tone of her voice, and it settles my ruffled feathers. "But you came all this way to make sure that she was safe. Treating you like that is disrespectful and ungrateful."

There was, but I'm not going to say it to this ethereal woman. "Where are we going?" I repeat.

"Upstairs. It seemed like a good idea to put some distance between the two of you in case she—" Aoibheall shoots a cautious look at me this time "—decides that you are in her path again."

That was a nice way of saying 'in case she decides to shove you over'. I had gotten the impression that I'd been a mere annoyance, but something has changed since Laura came out of the club. "That is very thoughtful of you. Thank you."

"And I'm not a terrible employer," she adds as she continues up the stairs. "I just have a short temper. Naoise has known me for so long that they know how to deal with me."

"It's still not right," I say. "Your employees have the right to a non-hostile working environment. Snapping at them and saying that's just because you have a temper really isn't on."

"We're not your normal working environment," says Aoibheall, and I'm about to ask her what she means when we're at the top of the stairs, and she opens the door to an office. Office itself is completely normal, wouldn't look out of place in the library where I work, but the view... It looks out across the club and my gaze can't help but be drawn to the figures beyond the window.

Aoibheall follows my eyes and stalks over and draws the curtain. "You haven't signed the non-disclosure agreement," she explains, almost apologetically. "Without that, I can't let you watch."

Of course she thinks that I just want to watch. I walk in here with my glasses and my cardigan, and everything about me screams good girl. I've *always* been the good girl. Always been the one to follow the rules and do as I was told and try and stop my sister getting into trouble.

My sister, who'll do what she pleases, and damn the consequences.

When is it *my* turn to have some fun?

When do *I* get to do more than just watch?

The silence in the room is weighted. There's depth to it, on both sides, and Aoibheall looks at me with unabashed curiosity.

"Give me the agreement," I say. There's not the slightest tremor in my voice, but my insides are churning. What am I doing?

She picks a form off the table, and a pen, but doesn't hand it over. "I need to tell you something first."

"What?"

"I'm not mortal." She doesn't couch her words in flowery language, or even soften it. "I'm fae. One of the Tuatha Dé Danann."

The words sit between us and I grasp at them.

Fae.

Tuatha Dé Danann.

The old Gods of Ireland that make up our history and our legends.

I don't take the pen.

You don't mess with the fae. That's the one thing that you know, being brought up in Ireland. Even though most people don't believe in their existence—dismiss the legends and stories for children—we still don't mess with the fae. There are old fairy forts dotted about the country and they're left well alone.

"What does signing this agreement do?" I ask.

She looks taken aback, and slightly pleased. "You don't trust me."

"You just told me that you're fae; I've read enough books in my time to know that you aren't exactly known for your trustworthiness."

Her eyes flash and there's something behind them, something grounded in pure anger, that makes her seem a little less ethereal. "Because mortals are known for their trustworthiness."

I pull out the chair by the desk and sit down in it heavily. "Fine, you don't like us. So why allow us in the club?"

"It's good for business," she says, as if parroting someone else's words. "If I had my way, we'd host fae and immortals, and no one else. But apparently that's not quite entertaining enough."

"We're more than entertainment." I'm bristling, unhappy with the way she's characterising us, even though I don't exactly disagree with her. Not about mortals being entertainment, but about the trustworthiness. I've been bitten too many times to doubt the honesty in that assertion.

"You might be." She looks directly at me then, and I don't have to force myself to meet her gaze. Usually I have to really concentrate to make eye contact—like I did earlier—but in this moment, I don't have to. It feels easy.

That should have been my first warning.

"How about we make a verbal agreement?" I say. "One that is witnessed."

"Legally we have to…" her voice trails off, and those green eyes deepen in colour, as if they're windows to an actual forest. "I would give you my word, as Aoibheall, Queen of Clare."

County Clare is a long way from here; I wonder why she hasn't gone home, but I trust her as much as I trust any fae. More so, because she doesn't seem like she'd lie to me about how she feels or what she'll do.

There's a knock on the door and Naoise is back. "Your sister has left." They address me, and I'm suddenly beset by the fact that I'd forgotten about Laura in the wake of the revelations. "If you'd like me to call you a taxi?"

"I've been invited to stay for the evening." They look taken aback and shoot a glance at Aoibheall. "Then I can get the paperwork—"

"We're going to make a verbal agreement, a promise of sorts."

Their eyebrows raise so high that they get lost in Naoise's bangs.

Bangs. A fae with bangs.

"Are you sure…?" Their voice trails off and they shake their head at Aoibheall's look. "Two centuries trapped behind the Veil, and you're going to risk it all. For what?"

There's a small part of me that wants to apologise, shut up, and head back home. To leave the lure of all this behind me and go back to my mundane life.

Aoibheall stares at me, and there's heat in her eyes that I

can't quite decipher. It could be desire, it could be anger. But it makes me feel alive.

"What do you wish for me to promise?"

I think, hard. "That for tonight you will respect my safewords and ensure that you are the only one to touch me."

4

———————

Aoibheall

Promises are tricksy things.

The fae rarely make promises, for if we do, they must be kept, and so their wording are careful things.

"I, Aoibheall, Queen of Clare, do swear that until sunrise tomorrow morning, I shall respect your safewords of..." I pause to let Lizzie fill in the gaps.

"Red, yellow and green."

"...red, yellow and green. And I will not allow you to be coerced into a scene with anyone other than me." I can feel the vow sealing itself beneath my skin, settling in until the words almost choke me with their chains. I don't make vows. Haven't done for centuries. And yet there's something about this woman that intrigues me. I want to undo her, and make her flame.

"That's not exactly what I said," she points out, "but I understand the changes that you have made, and why."

There needs to be nothing vague in our promise, and I

haven't manipulated my words in a way she hasn't seen either, almost careless in my kindness.

Naoise looks between us, and I can feel their curiosity rise.

"Your turn," I say. "What promise will you make me?"

She blinks behind those spectacles of hers, and I'm shot through with a curiosity of my own. How will she look when I unwrap her, when I set her above all, to be marvelled at in her freedom?

"I promise to safe out when I need to, to be honest with you about my desires... and my fears. Until sunrise."

"Until sunrise." I'm wishing sunrise away, long before the sun can even consider rising.

Naoise scoffs, and doesn't shrink back when I turn my gaze on them. "I'm saying nothing."

"Good."

As they leave, Lizzie gets to her feet and fidgets with the corner of the cloak-like cardigan she has draped around her. "What now?"

What now indeed.

I don't play with mortals. I don't usually play with anyone. I stand on the dais and watch over the club, keeping an eye on all that occurs, making sure that safewords are being respected. Watching the fae who escaped the Veil with us take full advantage of their freedom.

My sister brought her banshees with her, and they love to play and scene and watch. I... I don't really have anyone. I put my trust in mortals, long ago, and now my home thrives without me. They have forgotten that I was ever theirs, they were ever mine, and so this club is as much a limbo as life behind the Veil was.

Lizzie is still waiting for me to answer.

"What do you want to do?" I ask. "You want to watch?"

She flushes, and I expect her to say something about voyeurism, about watching those below. "I'm fed up of watching everyone else enjoy themselves. I want to enjoy *myself*. And I want you to make me."

Blood rushes through my veins, heating at her words. "You want me to force you?"

She doesn't like that word, but she doesn't deny it. "I've never taken my pleasure the way my sister has, never owned it. I'm not sure I even know how to. So, if you wouldn't mind taking charge, and yes, I suppose I want you to force pleasure from me, I'd be very grateful." Lizzie's mask is back, all prim and proper, as if she isn't asking me to ruin her.

"You'll need to say what you want," I tell her. "Voice those desires out loud. Otherwise how can I know what it is that you *truly* want?"

The only sound in the office is of her swallowing. "I can do that." She doesn't sound sure, and the words sound tight and contained, as if she's a violin who's been strung slightly too tightly. I don't want her to snap.

Not yet.

"And when I ask you what you want, you'll answer."

Her chin lifts in slight defiance. "I did promise."

"Fine," I say. "Follow me."

There is a door in the office that leads out onto the balcony above the club. No one else comes up here, not even Clíodhna—my sister prefers to be down there, amongst the people—and it feels odd having someone in this space that is so completely my own.

From here, Lizzie can see things that the kinksters below us can't. The small collection of books on a table by my chair, for when I can't be bothered with work, but I also don't want to be 'on'. There's a wall that hides certain details, and a throne. But it is still a dais. There are steps that lead down from a door in the wall, all the way to the main floor of the club.

I stalk over to the edge, snap my fingers, and some fae runs up the stairs as fast as they can. "Two waters."

"Yes, Queen Aoibheall." He scurries back down the steps and I turn to see Lizzie's nervousness give way to bemusement.

"You know I'm not calling you Queen," she says. "We're in the Republic of Ireland and we're more than a bit wary of monarchy."

"You don't have to call me anything," I tell her. "You just have to do as you're told."

A shiver runs over her body and I long to follow it with my hands, but she is still wearing all of those layers.

"Get undressed," I say, and turn my back on her as I take the two glasses of water from the fae who's back at the top of the stairs. I can feel her hesitation behind me, and I kind of hope she doesn't follow my orders. I want her to feel everything this evening, and I want to be the one to make that happen for her.

5

———————

Lizzie

She hasn't even touched me yet and I feel like I'm alight.

I like that she doesn't question my need to be forced, to have control and decision-making stripped away from me. I don't even know what I want, mainly because I don't know what it is I don't know. And I certainly don't know how to go about finding out. And it feels like Aoibheall has no qualms about making me do the things I long to try.

"You are not undressed," she says, not turning around. She lifts one glass to her mouth, and I watch as she gulps water. "Come here."

Slowly, I walk towards where she stands, looking out over all the people playing in her club. It's not as dimly lit as I thought, but the lighting is strategically placed, and there is a hum of activity below us. Every now and then, someone sees Aoibheall on the dais, and they bow their head, nodding their respect.

She turns to me, and her hair that seemed almost icy before, now feels like a white-hot flame. "Strip, Lizzie, before I make you."

I don't know how she'd make me, but from the look in her eyes, I'm not sure I'd enjoy it. A frisson of excitement runs through me and my hands move to discard my cardigan.

My clothes are dowdy, sure, but I've never really minded that before. People don't pay you much attention when you're dowdy, as if you're beneath even taunts. I'll take that over vicious words any day, but Aoibheall doesn't see my clothes. When her eyes sweep my body, it's as if she's looking past the layers, past skin even, into my very soul.

It's unnerving in the best kind of way.

"I'm bored," she declares. "You're taking too long."

Her hand reaches out and tugs me until I almost fall into her. I'm short, my head barely making her breasts, and my softness presses up against her. She has softness too, that's disguised by the dress she wears. "I'm going to rip your clothes from you," Aoibheall says. Her words are harsh, but she pauses, as if waiting for my response. I don't know if I want to dare her to do so, or want to feign reluctance.

"Green," I whisper, giving her the confirmation she needs.

Her nails catch on my skin lightly as she gathers the neckline of my top in both hands and I can't help the sharp in-breath that I take. Her grin is wicked, and her eyes sparkle with a delight that isn't quite kind.

When she tugs, the material is torn in two instantly, tearing in a clean line down my front. Aoibheall is stronger than she looks. That knowledge warms me, just as her eyes do when they realise that I'm not wearing anything beneath my top.

When people use words like curvy to describe women, they mean voluptuous. They mean the kind of hourglass woman who wouldn't out of place on a 1950s pin-up poster. There's nothing wrong with women like that—I'm a *big* fan of women like that—but that's not me. The only voluptuousness that I can claim lives in my hips and my arse. My breasts are small, so small that wearing a bra seems like a waste of time and fabric, and I'm definitely what one would call bottom heavy.

Aoibheall doesn't care. She stares at my breasts and my hardening nipples, and then spits out words like bullets. "You like this."

It's not a question, but I answer it as if it is. "Yes."

"Tell me what you want, Lizzie."

"I want your mouth on me."

She hasn't kissed me yet, but she doesn't hesitate before leaning all the way down and claiming a nipple with her lips. She sucks and nips and *fuck* that feels good. I try to hold back the noises I'm longing to make and she bites me. Not hard enough to draw blood, or even to bruise, but hard enough to ground me in the present.

"Ow!" I snap at her. "That hurt!"

"Really? I wasn't sure I was going hard enough, seeing as you weren't making any noise."

She's calling me out on my bullshit, and I love and hate it in equal measure. "Fuck you," I say, and a smile crawls across her face.

"Patience, I'm getting there." Then she steps back and the cool air against the tip of my nipple makes me shiver. "Step forward." Aoibheall gestures towards the edge of the balcony. I'm topless. If I walk there, everyone will... everyone will see me. Just as I am.

Step by tentative step, I move closer until I can see the

throng of people below. They're not all looking up at me, but some of them are, and the knowledge makes me wet.

"Lean over," she says, and indicates with her arms what she wants me to do. I copy, arms leaning on the top of the wall and my tiny titties swinging slightly beneath me.

I can feel her fiddling with the latch on my skirt, and then it falls away, the material brushing my legs like a caress as it drops.

I *am* wearing knickers, although not for long as her fingers rend them in two.

"Whoops," she says, clearly not sorry at all. Then she leans forward so that I can feel her long hair caressing my back, and whispers in my ear. "Don't you look pretty. Do you think that they agree?"

I force my head upwards and the eyes staring back at me... they're almost overwhelming. I'm suddenly reminded of the fact that I am one of maybe a handful of mortals here tonight; that the people in this club aren't really people at all. They're the fae, and I've read enough stories to know that what the fae want, the fae get.

Aoibheall must sense me stiffen, because she places a hand flat against my back, curving over my spine. "Remember my vow? No one touches you. Tonight you are mine."

6

____

Aoibheall

The woman is drenched, the material of her underwear sodden, and I want to fill her with my fingers now, damn it. But not touching her is starting to drive her slightly crazy.

Lizzie needs this.

I understand that now.

She's spent her whole life being good, being what everyone else expects her to be, and she's tired of it. If Lizzie wants a night of living for herself, then she shall have it.

Her hair is short, bobbed, but I can still entangle my fingers in it, fisting tightly until I know it almost hurts. Her wince is good, it means that she's here.

Performing like this, up on the dais, isn't something I've done before, or at least, not with another person. I suppose I'm always performing.

Lizzie, though, the sight of her, bent over before me is whipping up the crowd into a near frenzy. I can feel their lust, their desires. Some of the fae below copy her stance, bending over couches, and watch her face as they're fucked roughly from behind with straps or dicks or fingers.

I run my hands down across her back, and then from hip to hip. They can drink their fill, watch her as much as they like, but I wasn't exaggerating when I spoke. Tonight, she belongs to me.

"What would you have me do with you?" I ask her.

She pauses, and I can almost hear her brain running through a list of acceptable answers. I lift my hand and bring it down sharply on her right arse cheek. The crack of the slap mingles with the cry she emits. "Stop curating your answers. Instinctual answers only please."

"I told you." I can hear the tension in her voice; she's pissed. "I. Don't. Know."

Her answer gives me pause. I can sense that she's not lying, but Lizzie's frustration is palpable. "Explain."

"I don't know what I'd have you do to or with me, because I don't know what the options are. I know some of them, but you own a sex club, I'm sure you've far more interesting solutions."

That's true.

"What're your safewords?" I know what they are, but I'm checking she remembers.

"Red, yellow, green."

"Okay then." I turn my head and look down the stairs, catching the eye of the fae who brought me water earlier. Clicking my fingers brings him running. I mutter my order in his ear, and he nods and disappears.

I sit in the chair close to the wall and watch her. I'm sat to the side, so I can observe her face, and whilst she seems frustrated, she hasn't moved from the position I told her to take up.

"Feet further apart," I say and she obeys instantly.

"Doesn't seem like you need forcing to me." She turns her head to look at me then and her glare makes me laugh. "Don't worry, I'm going to make you take it, but only after you beg me for it."

Her mouth drops open, just a tiny bit, and I can see the effect that my words are having on her. Brown irises soften and for an instant, she looks for all the world like she wants to smile, as if the way I'm speaking to her is the kindest anyone has ever been.

I know that I'm not nice—I'm a fae queen; we're not known for being nice—but I can do this one thing. I can give her this gift.

The fae is back, panting slightly as he stands at the top of the stairs, offering me a basket of fruit. I take it, and dismiss him with a wave of my hand.

"What's that—"

"Eyes front." My words cut across her question and again she obeys instinctively. There's something delicious about getting to see someone so clearly made for submission experience it for the first time.

I look back down at the basket and see what he's brought me. Apples and quinces and peaches and melons, and such an array of berries that I'm tempted to praise him. I won't though. I am Queen and this is my due.

"I'm going to paint you with fruit," I say. "I'm going to crush berries and peaches against your skin until you're dripping everywhere—and not just from your cunt."

She reddens at that, but stays where she is.

I take a finger and run it down her back, letting the nail score a red mark that will fade before the evening is out. "Let me make you complicit in your own downfall: would you like me to lay you out on a table? Or truss you up?"

The muttered answer is so quiet I can't hear it.

"I can't hear you!" I say, singsong-style. "Try again Lizzie, and this time—" I lower my voice until it's almost a threat "—I'd best hear your choice."

"Table please."

"Excellent. Time for a feast!"

I wave a hand and use some of the extraneous magic that's hovering in the air. Casting spells isn't usually my style, but I don't want to wait any longer than I have to, to see her all laid out in front of me. The magic takes the small side table and glamours it big.

But when she turns around, Lizzie eyes it nervously. "That... that doesn't look very sturdy."

It looks perfectly fine to me, but from the way she hugs herself, I realise that it might be the sturdiest table in the world, but with thin legs, Lizzie is going to worry about it. I wave my hand again, and the glamour shifts.

"But now I *know* it's not real." Her eyes look panicked and I don't intend to let her flail if I can help it.

Two quick steps forward and I fist my hand in her hair, and tug until her head falls back and she bares her neck to me. Someone whoops downstairs but I don't give them a second glance. "You are mine, Lizzie Byrne, and I look after what is mine."

Her breathing is shallow, tiny little breaths that sound like whispers of desire. With my spare hand I bracket her throat gently, and she leans into it, choking herself.

I tighten my hand slightly and in one movement lift her into the air and onto the table. Fae strength does have its advantages.

She doesn't protest, but rather unfurls like a flower, stretching herself out until I can see all of her.

Her belly is bountiful, and her hips are rounded, and her small breasts are enticingly pert. But when she avoids my gaze this time, it is not due to the autism. "Look at me," I order, and she does.

Dark brown eyes stare up at me soulfully, and she blinks once, long lashes kissing her face.

"I think you need to see what I see," I say, and conjure up a mirror just as she says, "Yellow!"

I drift the mirror to the side, and turn it away from her. "Lizzie?"

"I just... I won't be able to turn off my brain if I'm watching myself. I'll be so hyperaware of everything, and just now, I was able to sink into my body, to lose myself. I want to be able to do that again, and too many sensory inputs..." She sits up on the table and reaches out for me.

I don't shy away.

"Please, Aoibheall, give me this?"

The mirror vanishes as her hand touches my cheek. My in-breath seems loud, and her hands are soft, the soft touch of a scholar. I don't know whether to turn my head and kiss her palm, or bite her. Frozen, I stand absolutely still, until she smiles wistfully and lays back down.

"Thank you, Aoibheall."

People don't thank me. They don't see past the outer layer of fae queen long enough to be gentle with me, to be soft with me, and Lizzie? Lizzie is all of those things.

7

———

Lizzie

I am not afraid of my body. This is not about the fact that I am fat, a fact that I am very well aware of. It's about sensory overload. I want to do everything Aoibheall wishes of me, but the sensations of food on my skin, it might be too much.

She looks at me for a long time.

I can't read that look. I don't think that she's annoyed with me, for her gaze has softened slightly, and there's the hint of a smile playing about her lips.

"Too many sensory inputs? Maybe I should blindfold you then."

I shiver involuntarily.

When she smiles this time, there is no doubting it; there's a cruelness in smiles like this, that promises wicked pleasure, and some pain too. I want that. I want the double-sided sting of desire.

Producing a scarf, she offers it to me with a question. "Do you trust me?"

I consider her for a moment, and nod.

The scarf is silken, smooth as it glides across my face. A hand lifts my head so that Aoibheall can tie it. Not too tight, but I doubt that this will move unless she, or I, move it ourselves.

The world quietens.

It doesn't really, I can still hear the sounds of the club below the dais, but here, in this bubble, it has quietened. I have quietened.

My heartbeat slows, settling, even as I await the next steps. There's a serenity in this waiting. I can't see what's happening, I can't see what she's going to do to me and the inevitability of it all settles into my bones.

I am hers.

When she said it before, I felt *something*, deep in my gut, resonate with the words, but now I truly believe them. Aoibheall could levitate me in the air, and I'd let her.

She moves around me. I can hear the whisper of her skirts, and her long hair brushes against y arm as she circles me. Eventually she comes to a stop, somewhere near my head—I think—and I strain to hear what she's doing.

You'd think that with my sight restricted, my hearing would sharpen, but it's not like that. So when she presses a berry against my lips, it takes me by surprise.

It's a raspberry, sharp in its sweetness, and she crushes it against my lips before pushing it into my mouth, the pad of her thumb pressing against my mouth insistently. I swallow the raspberry, and leave my mouth slightly open.

Next up is a peach that she gets me to take a bite of. It's ripe and the juices run down my chin. I don't get more than one bite though, because then she lifts it away. I make a noise of frustration, because I like peaches, and then I feel it. The juice from the peach dripping onto my skin. There's a stickiness to it that would usually upset me, bother me, but it's not on my hands—somehow Aoibheall realises to keep my hands free of juice. Instead it drips over each breast, my nipples puckering and tightening as the drops fall, until they ache with wanting to be touched.

I can't bear it. Although I can, and I will.

My determination not to falter is strong though, and I keep still and silent.

Aoibheall's hot mouth shocks me out of my silence though, drawing my nipple in and sucking on it, until she tugs with teeth.

That shocks a gasp out of me.

The contrast between the wetness of her mouth, and the cool sticky peach juice sets my head spinning and I moan.

"That's it," she says. "I want to hear you. If I'm feasting on you, I want to know that despite everything, you long for it too."

I clench my jaw shut and shake my head, but when her hand hovers above my throat until I can feel the heat from her skin above mine, I mutter out green.

"Green?" she mocks. "Green? You want more?"

"Yes, damn it," I say, and her laugh is shocked and throaty. She delights in my defiance, I can sense that. I'm somewhat delighted myself. I wouldn't usually bite back like this. I might deliver a sharp putdown at work, if people are breaking library rules, but other than that I usually take it.

Laura's always been the one to be naughty.

"I like being naughty," I say out loud, and I can't see her and she doesn't say a thing, but I can almost hear her smile. "And you said I should beg for it."

"You want to beg for more fruit? They're ripe and juicy." She runs a hand across my belly, and up until she pinches my nipple, chuckling at my hiss.

"That's not what I was begging for."

"But it's what you're getting," she says, and a deluge of berries hit me from above. She's right, they're ripe, and if I had to guess, she's squashed them because as they hit my body, they don't just bounce off, they hit and run down the side, leaving sticky fruit stains.

All at once I want to see myself, want to see my body painted with the colours of bright fruit. For once, I don't mind being a sticky mess, because it feels like more than mess.

It feels like art.

Aoibheall is an artist and I her canvas, wet and sticky and desperate for more.

More berries hit my skin, and this time, her fingers press them into me, walk them across my tits and hips and tum.

She doesn't touch me where I'm wettest though, and I'm torn between longing to be sticky *there*, and needing her mouth to suck intensely on my clit like it did my nipples.

"I want to see," I mutter, and the blindfold is ripped away, tugged up and off my head and I'm beset by light that makes me blink and almost shrink away.

I look up and see the back of the mirror, plain and dark.

"Are you sure?" she asks, and I nod in answer.

"Words, Lizzie."

"Green."

When the mirror turns around I'm taken aback by how I look. My lips are dyed a deep pink by the raspberry, and my hair looks wild, but it's the rest of me that I can't stop looking at. Pink and purple and blue streaks across my body, decorating me in a way that I couldn't have even imagined. It looks like a sunset on my body, as if *I'm* the sunset, aflame and desperate for all that the world promises.

All that Aoibheall promises.

I see her then, reflected in the mirror, her imposing figure more of a comfort than a threat. She's looking down at me, so she doesn't realise that I can see the kindness in those green eyes, captured on the mirror that she has hovering above me.

"I look..." I don't have the words to describe how I look. Abundant would cover it best, I think.

She doesn't finish my sentence for me, but lets the unfinished phrase hang in the air between us. With a wave of her hand, she dismisses the mirror and I see it almost fold into the air and disappear.

"Come Lizzie," she says. "I know what I wish to do with you next."

8

———————

Aoibheall

I don't clean the juice from Lizzie's body. I like how it decorates her, marks her.

She's mine, and anyone looking at her will know it.

It's been years since I've felt this possessive over someone, centuries even. Not since Dubhlaing threw away two hundred years of happiness with me for a moment of ego on the battlefield.

It's weird, to have that thrum of desire running through my veins, and not have it unpinned by distrust and anger. I might have felt anger at the beginning, but now it's dissipated. Now all I feel is my desire for her.

I know what I wish to do next, and I know that it's a test of some sorts. Perhaps it is not fair, not to tell Lizzie what I am doing, what I am testing, but if I warn her it would skew her response.

Taking her hand, I pull her to sitting. "How would you like to be a statue?" I ask her.

"I don't want to be turned into a literal statue," she says, her words careful.

I wave my free hand. "Not a literal statue, I want you to act like a statue for me, to hold still in whatever position I place you in. Will you promise me?"

Her eyes sharpen at the word promise, and she's smart enough to guess that there's something that I'm not telling her. "I won't promise," she says. "But I can try."

Trying is good enough for me, and I like that she didn't make a spur of the moment promise without working out whether or not she could keep it.

She swings her legs over the side of the table, and as she stands up, I dismiss the glamour. Lizzie makes a strangled noise, and I grin at her. The table is back to being the delicate little side table it always was. "Magic," I say, and am rewarded with a gurgle of a laugh.

I beckon her towards the front of the dais, and point out across the room. "I'm going to make them all watch you, all worship your beauty."

Her face screws up, just slightly, and I won't have that, I won't have her doubting herself. My hand on her throat, I pull her towards me. "Do not doubt me, Lizzie, and do not doubt what I see."

She huffs out a smile, and I captured it with my mouth.

I kiss her.

My first kiss in centuries.

Her lips are soft, and her mouth pliable, and she melts beneath my touch, as if I'm flame against ice. Her knees almost give way, but I catch her to myself, not caring what the juices painting her skin might do to my dress.

Gods, I could get drunk on her kisses.

She gives of herself so freely, taking my kiss at first, and then returning it with a fiery passion that ignites emotions that have long since been buried.

Tugging her lower lip between my teeth, I suck, our noses rubbing against one another, and her tongue darts out, tentatively exploring my mouth. It makes *me* melt.

I'm faintly aware of cheers below us, and when we break apart, breathing heavily, I see my sister out of the corner of my eye. She's smiling, and I almost shove Lizzie away from me.

My relationship with Clíodhna, even after all these years, is odd. My sister stirs up feelings of resentment, even though it's been centuries since she turned me into a cat. Her approval comes at a cost, makes me doubt the validity of my decisions, and my instinct is to send Lizzie away.

But when I look at her, she's seeing me. Actually seeing me and my anxiousness, and this subby mortal actually asks me if I need to take a break. "You can safe out too," she says.

I know that. Technically I do, but I've never safed out before, and I don't intend on starting now. I go to kiss her again, but she places her hand atop my chest and I feel it through the layer of fabric that separates us.

"Yellow," she says.

A pit in my stomach opens, and I'm freefalling down. I want to kiss her, but if she doesn't want that, if she wants only pleasure, then I can deliver on that. It'll just make me feel empty and—

Her hands are cradling my face, and she's had to go onto her tiptoes to do so. "Aoibheall, I'm right here. Come back to me."

I look anywhere but at her, until she says, firmly. "Eyes on me please."

My eyes flick up, and meet hers.

"Now, I don't know what's wrong, but something isn't right."

"I'm perfectly alright—"

"Stop it," she says, the words bursting out of her in a waterfall. "You're not alright. I don't know why, or how, but something has shifted and you're not alright."

I stare at her.

She shakes her head in frustration. "Just because I can't read people doesn't mean I can't tell when something has changed. Something has changed and you either explain, or we stop."

Lizzie is perfectly serious, I can see it in the set of her jaw and the determination in her eyes. "My sister is watching us," I mumble.

"Oh," her face clears. "Yes, I can imagine that would be rather odd. Would you prefer we move somewhere else?"

"It's not that," I flush, and I know that the patchy red in my cheeks isn't attractive, and all at once I'm feeling self-conscious as well as off-kilter. "She's looking pleased, that we're doing this. She's happy for me and that makes me feel... weird."

Lizzie's face scrunches up. I like watching her think and react. Since we've been on the dais, she hasn't hidden how she's feeling; I can read it, emotions written across her face. She's clearly confused.

"You don't want your sister to be happy for you?"

"How would you feel if Laura was happy for you?" Her face shutters instantly and I regret my words, wish that I could pull them back, anything to stop her from putting up a wall between us both. "I'm sorry, I didn't mean—"

"No no," she says softly. "That's a fair comparison. If I'm completely honest with myself, I don't think that Laura really considers me at all, other than when she needs a lift somewhere, or help with something. I'm too boring for my sister."

I step back and let myself drink in the vision that is Lizzie, painted with fruit juices. "I don't see anyone boring."

Her smile is small, but it rings true. "Thank you. And I think perhaps you should just accept that maybe your sister is actually happy for you."

I turn and look out, finding Clíodhna, meeting her eyes. The pain there is reflected in my own. I wasn't happy for her when she first played with Janet; I was livid. So angry that I triggered the three trials that left iron-branded scars on my sister's hands. I don't know if I can ever truly forgive myself for that.

She won't trigger trials for Lizzie and me, I know that, and since the Morrígan respond so strongly to Janet's trials, none of the fae who have taken mortal lovers since have been forced to face them either, but it doesn't stop me from feeling guilty.

Lizzie

One of the things I struggle with the most about my autism, is not being able to read people. It's brutal. People get frustrated when you ask if they're okay, over and over and over, because you know that something is wrong, but heaven forbid your brain actually process what that something is. So I'm grateful that Aoibheall has answered my query, that she's trying to explain what's made her feel so guilty.

I know she wants to do more things with me, that she wants to kiss me, but I feel weird about her burying her hurt and losing herself in my body.

I'd rather she face it, and then we return to our pleasure together, both of us fully present.

I glance over to where Aoibheall's sister stands, a short woman who seems very human by her side. "She has a human lover?"

Aoibheall nods. "Yes, Janet. She's... she's an acceptable mortal."

"Are most mortals unacceptable then?"

The look she shoots me burns. It's anguished and I am filled with hate for whoever put it in her eyes. "Mortals are renowned for being fickle and disloyal."

"That's a bit harsh," I say, and then think of Laura, shoving me to the floor. "Maybe true sometimes, but not of all mortals. There's good in us."

"There's good in *you*," she says, and walks towards me so quickly that I find myself backing up until I hit the wall of the office behind me. "There's good in you Lizzie."

Her eyes search mine and I blink away, suddenly overwhelmed by the intensity of her stare. "I try my best," I say primly, and want to kick myself.

A low chuckle reverberates through her. I can feel it where her hand cups my cheek, and feel an echoing reverberation in my clit.

"I'm here," she says. "I'm here Lizzie, and you're mine. So for tonight, let me make you feel everything."

I believe her. She is back, fully present in this moment with me, and I kiss her impetuously, reaching up to press my lips to hers.

She picks me up and does something so that it feels like I'm standing on a stool. The solidness beneath my feet reassures me that I'm safe, and it's only when I look down that I realise that I'm hovering in the air.

"Aoibheall!" I say, but she's back to kissing me.

"It's okay," she says. "I've got you."

And I give her my trust and try not to think about the fact that there is technically a good foot and a half of air between my feet and the floor. She kisses me some more, before stepping back and leaving me hanging there, suspended in mid-air.

I should be more freaked out, I really should. I should be

jumping down from this spot and demanding how she did it, or why she's left me here, but I don't.

Instead, I just wait.

Aoibheall grins at me, a smirk that I've come to recognise as a sign that she's got a plan of sorts up her sleeve. "How do you like your pedestal?"

"What?"

"I've put you on a pedestal," she says, repeating herself.

I'm not really sure what her point is, but I guess that she's going to elucidate. And of course she does.

"You've spent so much of your life being the 'good one', up on this pedestal, and now you've chosen to step off it and get mucky with the rest of us."

"Literally," I add, glancing down to wear my stomach has been painted with fruit.

"Exactly, but this is a choice. *Your* choice." She takes a step towards me, and reaches out to hold my chin so I can't look away from her. "You want to get dirty, Lizzie? Then step down off that pedestal and I will ruin you."

Meeting her eyes, as I can at this height for once, I scoff. "You want to ruin me? You in your fancy dress?" I'm half goading her now. As prim and proper as I am, she's all leashed energy, held back. I don't want her to hold back; I want her to let loose on me, and I don't think she will unless I push her.

She meets my eyes and smiles. "You really do want me to make you."

"I really do," I reply. "I want you to take me, Aoibheall, and force pleasure from me that I've only ever imagined." Glancing down, I see that her hands are trembling, shaking, and I can't tell whether it's with suppressed need, or leftover from the emotions that beset her just moments ago. "We don't have to though." My words are hurried, but no less truthful, for all that. "If you're not sure." Do I need this? Absolutely, but not at the expense of someone else's comfort.

Her eyes flash a weird bright green, so different from the tranquil forest I've seen so far, but I don't recoil. I'm fascinated. *She* is fascinating. "Oh I'm sure," she says. "Step down off that pedestal and see how sure I am."

"Undress first." My voice is steady, steadier than I feel. "I want us on more of an even footing."

She doesn't say anything, just starts unlacing the front of her dress. It's not a corset, so her breasts don't suddenly drop when it comes apart. They're bigger than mine, rounded and soft looking, with peaks that are dusted with pink. The lacing finishes at the waistband and then she lets the skirt drop completely, before stepping out of her dress entirely. There's no shyness in her whatsoever, as if she knows how incredible she looks, and takes my awed silence as her due. But then she laughs, and there's awkwardness there. "You're staring Lizzie."

"I mean, yeah. Have you seen you?"

"You say that whilst elevated before me on a pedestal, all bountiful abundance, the ultimate temptation?" Her laugh is short, but warm with promise. "Stay there as long as you like, Lizzie; I can wait you out."

She drops to her knees before me, and I'm taken aback. This wasn't what I expected. Inching forwards, she licks her lips. "Do you know how much I'm dying to taste you? How much I long to dip my mouth and taste your nectar?" She's edging closer to me now, and I can feel her breath on the inside of my thighs. I want her—no, I *need* her to touch me there.

Aoibheall's kissed me, she's touched my back, my tits, even spanked my arse once, but she's kept away from where my clit's been throbbing insistently.

"Please," I beg. "Please, Aoibheall."

She looks up at me, green eyes shining. "Only if you step down."

10

———————

Aoibheall

I've never debased myself like this.

I've had other fae prostrate themselves before me as I step over—and sometimes on—them, but I've never gotten on my knees for someone. It's just not something I'd ever do.

And yet here I am, waiting for Lizzie to step off her pedestal as if she's some beautiful statue come to life.

This feels different, this kind of play. I'm still in charge, still the one who's making the decisions, but I'm also half-worshipping this mortal who fell into my life just a few short hours ago. The colour dyeing her belly is as vivid as the intensity of my longing for her. She's playing with me, teasing, and I'm actually allowing it—partly because she's cute when she's defiant, and partly because I now that when she steps down, she's mine.

I'm a fae queen. I know what power sex has, what it can bestow upon mortals who take fae lovers. And I know how it can ruin them, make them feel invincible.

I'm temptation personified, and yet she doesn't view me like that. I'm not the one who tempted her, even though I am encouraging her. *She* is the one who is choosing this. That's why it's important that she steps down off this pedestal of her own accord. I want her to want this.

I need her to want this.

Her fingers reach for me, caressing the top of my head and I close my eyes for a moment and revel in the sensations. She's not trying to pull me closer, though I can tell she wants to. Tilting my head, I look up at her, and she's got this half-smile on her face, as if she truly can't quite believe what she's seeing.

And then she steps down.

I grab her instantly round the waist, pulling her roughly until she's underneath me, all naked and soft and...

"Well, what do we have here?"

Curses fly from my mouth and I round on Medb with a ferocity that surprises all three of us on the dais. "What the fuck do *you* want?" I'm leaning over Lizzie, shielding her from Medb's gaze in a protective stance that I never took when I was with Dubhlaing.

Lizzie is as sensible as ever, and merely peeks her head under my shoulder and says cheerfully. "Oh hello. I don't suppose you could give us a moment, could you?"

I wait for the inevitable in-breath. Medb is stunning; it's foolish to deny it. Of the three fae queens who frequent the club she is the one that the clients lust over the most. They follow Clíodhna, they fear me and they desire Medb.

But Lizzie's voice doesn't change from that bright, friendly tone she's using, the tone that implies that she's not naked beneath me, about to have her brains fucked out, but rather that this is a perfectly normal and socially acceptable first meeting.

"But why would I give you a moment, when watching here is so much more fun?" She's not normally this much of an arse, but Medb has been bored lately. It explains why she thought it'd be a good idea to interrupt this scene. "The whole club is a-buzz about the little mortal whom Aoibheall's taken as a lover. I thought you were done with mortals, Aoibheall?" Her words are sharp, and I'm reminded of her cruel laughter when Dubhlaing died. I didn't cry—he didn't deserve my tears—but I felt sorrow nonetheless. Sorrow and anger.

"You'll get used to it," she'd said. "After the sixth husband, you don't even notice when they die."

I vowed then that I was done with mortals, and it feels like she's here, now, to remind me of it.

"Excuse me." Lizzie's bright tone has been replaced with a sharper one. "I made a request and I would appreciate if you'd respect it."

Medb laughs, a low throaty chuckle that threatens to turn my knees to jelly. She knows how to weaponise her wiles. Speaking of anyone else, that would be an insult. It sounded like the bitter remark of an old man who no woman would touch. But Maeve had spent centuries as a sovereign fae queen, bestowing kingship upon whoever she fucked, and so she'd learned to use that to her advantage. And in this moment, it looks like she was planning on using it against my Lizzie.

It wasn't going to work. If anything, it was going to piss Lizzie off more, which I would find highly entertaining.

But then Lizzie wriggles out from underneath me and stalks over to face off with Medb. That was not how this was supposed to go.

"Get out," she says, her words sharper than any inch of her, so sharp that they could wound. Medb goes to shrug them off, but Lizzie isn't finished. "I don't care if you were Ériu herself, you don't crash a private scene, and then mock the participants. It's bad manners, and you're clearly old enough by a couple of centuries to know better."

There's a prolonged silence in which I'm beginning to feel remarkably uncomfortable. Being blunt and forthright towards Medb is one thing, but invoking Ériu has been known to have some ever so unfortunate side effects. Even Medb is looking alarmed, as well as rather impressed at Lizzie's calling on the Goddess of Éire herself.

Lizzie is standing there, stark naked, hands on those delicious hips of hers, and I can't help but admire her behind. It's full and jiggles as she moves. I love a jiggle.

There's a scuffle from inside the office, and now Janet is at the door. "I really am sorry to interrupt, but the Clíodhna said something about—" Her eyes fall upon the tableau laid out before her. "Nope. Don't want to know. Don't want to—" Her words cut off again, and she's clearly trying to stop Clíodhna from coming in and interfering. My sister is surprisingly protective of me, for someone who once turned me into a cat.

Lizzie shoots a glance at me, and I realise that all of this is too much for her. Too many people in close proximity whilst she's naked and vulnerable.

I stand and draw myself up to my true height. "Leave," I say, and I imbue it with all the foreboding that I can. I've warned kings of their deaths in a friendlier tone than this. "Both of you need to leave now."

"Or what?" asks Medb, who clearly hasn't fully registered my tone.

"Or you'll join those nine husbands of yours," I say. Nine husbands married, nine husbands buried.

Janet proffers a tentative, "Perhaps if we just talk this all out ..."

"*No*." Her face whitens and she takes a step back. She rarely takes my threats this seriously, so I must look pretty fearsome.

"Come Janet," Medb says. "Let's leave Aoibheall to her mortal lover."

11

———————

Lizzie

The club is silent when they leave. Quieter than stunned silence, and when I peak my head over the edge of the dais, I see that the club has cleared out altogether.

"Everyone's left," I say.

"Good," she replies. "We don't need them here anyway." She looks worried as she looks at me. "I didn't scare you?"

"No," I say. "You didn't scare me."

"You need everyone to leave you alone though?"

"Everyone apart from you." I've known her mere hours, and yet she feels like next zero spoons to me, someone who doesn't take up energy to be around.

"What else do you need?"

I could do the sexy thing and say 'you', and we'd start up right where we left off, but I need a moment or two to recentre myself. "I don't suppose we could turn the lights off? Not all of them, just some of them. It feels super bright."

It's not bright, I know that, but sensory overwhelm

doesn't take that into account. I could be in the quietest room, and a pin dropping could set me off sometimes. And right now, I'm squinting at the lights above, and wanting the low lighting to drop even lower.

She doesn't even question my request, just opens the gate at the top of the dais and heads down the steps. The lights dim soon after, until there are only three lights left on. One where I am (though it's dimmed), one by the bar, and one on the stage where the St Andrew's Cross is. Aoibheall stands at the bottom of the stairs and waits for me to descend.

I'm still covered in fruit juice, though it doesn't feel sticky any longer, and I'm wet between my legs. And I want Aoibheall to take me. But I don't want any more interruptions. "Is anyone else going to try and strike up a conversation with you?" I ask, teasingly.

Aoibheall strides over to the door that links the main club to the reception and shoves it open. "Naoise, the club is closing for the rest of the night. Yes, you can go home, but please inform my sister."

"I'm standing right here." Her sister's voice sounds indignant but amused.

"Lizzie and I would like the place to ourselves for the rest of the night," says Aoibheall, as if she hasn't heard her sister. "Anyone interrupts me, and *they'll* spend the next decade as a cat."

There's a spluttering of laughter, but she's already closing the door and coming back to me.

"A cat?" I ask.

"Payback," she says. "Now are you coming down those stairs or not?"

It feels like I'm walking into the dark, taking steps into the depths of hell—if you even believe in such a thing. But

I'd go there a thousand times if Aoibheall were waiting at the bottom for me. She's luminous. Literally. Her hair floats around her, and it makes her look like Cate Blanchett's Galadriel—not nice welcoming Galadriel, but Galadriel on speed—only a smidgeon less terrifying.

When my foot steps off the last step, she's there, pulling me into her arms, and kissing me all over. Her mouth traces the line of my neck until she's nuzzling at my nape, and lean my head back and let myself moan the way that I've wanted to this whole time.

The sound echoes through the room and Aoibheall growls at the sound of it.

"I want to burn you up," she admits, "want to take you in my arms and have you so desperate for me that you're almost crying, and then I will set you aflame with pleasure."

"Go on then," I say, daring her. Extricating myself from her arms, I nip at her shoulder and she swipes at me jokingly.

"You little brat."

"You've yet to truly make me do anything," I taunt. "Do you really think you can?"

That bright green light is back in her eyes, and I'm reminded of the fae hunts of which I've read. There's something about her that reads predator, though I don't really feel in danger. She's sworn to protect me, to respect my safewords. I am safe for tonight, so tonight I will run.

"I know I can," she says, and with a click of her fingers, all of the lights go out.

My skin goosebumps, and I close my eyes, trying to hear for her in the dark. When she laughs, it's as if the laughter is coming from all around, like it's surrounding me. I duck down and crawl along on my hands and knees, feeling my way forward until I feel the edge of the stage. Standing myself up, I try to pull myself up onto it, but this is where being a shortarse really is a pain. I'm too small. I can't get enough purchase because my arms are reaching up, and this is frustrating.

I feel her breath on the back of my neck before she grabs me, swings me up into the air, and then places me on the edge of the stage, legs dangling down.

Another click of her fingers and she's luminous again. Hands slide up my legs to my knees and then coax them apart.

"I'm going to touch you," she says, "but you're not allowed to come. Do you understand?"

I nod, but that isn't good enough.

"Use your words Lizzie. And tell me what you want."

My words feel delicate, juddery on my tongue. "I want you to touch me. I want you to set me aflame."

"And?"

"And I want to wait until you tell me I can come."

I wait for her to say good girl, or offer me some such praise, but she doesn't. Aoibheall merely smirks. "You're green?"

Swallowing, I nod. "I'm green."

She stretches my legs open wide, wider than I expect, in such a swift movement that I grunt in surprise, and then she's on her knees again.

I don't know what it is I expect. Maybe tentative licking, a delicate finger running between my lips. She does neither of those things. She blows.

Cool air assaults my clit and I flinch. After all this time, after the fruit and the pedestal and the nakedness, all she has to do is blow on me to make me shudder. It's almost too much, and simultaneously not at all enough. I growl my frustration, and tug at her head, urging it closer.

She turns her head and nips my inner thigh and I stop moving.

"Red?" she asks, so in tune to my body, that she notices even the slightest change in my temperament.

"Yellow?" I say, and run my finger across the mark she's made. It's not bleeding, but the skin there is so thin that the bite felt sharper, sharper even than when she bit my nipple with more gusto than this. "No biting there, I don't think."

She kisses the spot then, lathing it with my tongue, and I moan. The heat of her mouth, fuck I need it on my clit.

"I need you on me," I say.

"Patience, Lizzie," she says. Good things come to those who wait."

12

———

Aoibheall

I want to heighten her pleasure, so I start small. Gentle brushes against her clit with air alone, no fingers or mouth, not yet. As I do, I run my hands up and over the swell of her hips, to where I painted her belly with fruit. I want more of the same, so summon another peach with a wave of my hand.

I bite into it and moan. "It tastes good, Lizzie. Sweet like nectar. Just like I know you'll taste."

She moans, the sound tinged with frustration, but I don't stop. I kiss her inner thigh, on that same spot, and let the juices from the peach drip down her leg before I trace it with my tongue. She shivers beneath my touch, and I revel in it, knowing that my gentle torture is having an effect.

I want to overwhelm her with it all.

As I lick down her thigh, I run my nails up the back of her calf and up her thigh. She's openly shivering now, little staccato movements that show how much she's enjoying this. Two fingers run across her pubic bone and then I curl my hand, separating my index and middle finger so that when I brush down between her legs, they miss her clit.

She groans, and makes a funny little noise at the back of her throat when I run my fingers of both hands down the tops of her thighs this time. Lizzie likes my nails, she squeaks when I use them, and when I pass her ankles I encircle them with my fingers, pressing the heels of my hands down.

The sound she makes then is different. It's not so much of a gasp or a moan, but rather a sigh, as if I've found the perfect way to undo her.

I've never massaged feet before, and I certainly don't know what I'm doing, but I apply more pressure and am rewarded with another sigh. Lizzie leans back on her wrists and meets my eyes.

"You like that." It's not a question.

She nods. "It quiets me." I'm not sure that's exactly what I'm aiming for, Lizzie's eyes urge me on, and this time there's a rumbly groan when I tighten my grip. "Like that," she says, and just for fun I lean forward and blow on her clit again.

It's hard to jump when your feet are being held firmly against the floor, and I feel Lizzie's entire body tighten up, as if the shock of the restraint is felt in her core. Her eyes widen and she nods. "Yes, Aoibheall," she gasps. "Please."

I might be restraining her, but my own restraint is shot, I lean forward and suck her clit into my mouth and am rewarded with a shouted curse. *Shout as loud as you like*, I think. *No one here will hear your screams of pleasure.*

The button is hard against my tongue as I flick it and she shudders.

"More," she whispers.

Is this the same woman who wanted me to make her? I tighten the suction around her clit and she almost sobs.

She's desperate for me, turning pleading eyes on me so intently that I have to fight not to give in.

"I'll give you more," I say, my words kissing her clit, "I'll give you more than you could ever handle, as long as you keep your promise."

"My promise?"

"You don't come until I say."

"Yes, Aoibheall," Lizzie says. "I don't come until you say."

I don't need any more moisture on my fingers, she's more than wet enough for me to slide two fingers. She is hot and wet and I curse as I fill her up.

Her laughter makes look up at her. "I'm the one being filled up, Aoibheall," she says. "I should be the one swearing."

I take that as a request, and slide out before ramming back in, hard. She gasps and falls back until she's lying flat on the stage, legs spread as I fingerfuck her. Her pussy is clenching around, tiny little spasms that indicate that her orgasm is approaching and I slow down instantly, and pinch her clit.

She jolts and swears at me. "What the fuck was that for?"

"I thought you weren't going to come until I say."

"I wasn't coming," she pleads, but we both know that she wasn't far off. "Please, Aoibheall, please."

This time I add a third finger as I fingerfuck her, and then a fourth, and she takes my fingers so easily, her pussy greedy for more. And she's keening now, begging me more, more more. My hand is upturned, my thumb brushing against her clit each time I enter her, and eventually I move it so it too is positioned at her entrance. I don't think she'll be able to take my whole fist, not this time at least, but she'll be able to take all five digits.

My left hand moves so that I'm circling her clit with my

thumb, long, movements that sync up with the thrusts of my fingers.

"More," she whispers again. "I can take it, Aoibheall, I promise."

I add my thumb and she opens for me and takes it all.

Her eyes are wide and I can see her fighting her release. "I'm trying," she gasps, "but I'm so close."

"That's okay," I say. "Because you're going to come for me Lizzie. You're going to come for me because you are mine, sweet Lizzie."

She shatters then, into a million pieces, with a sound that I feel in the very depths of me. Her body is tight and loose and I am standing, kissing her painted belly, my hair falling across her as she comes. Lizzie shakes and shakes, and when the cry dies away, her mouth is still open in a silent cry. Withdrawing from her, I clamber up onto the stage and pull her into my arms and hold her and rock her as she comes down.

"Well, wasn't that something?" says a voice.

13

———

Lizzie

I'm barely aware of what's going on, and it's only when Aoibheall's arms tighten around me, that I blearily raise my head to look. "I thought the club was closed?" I ask when I finally register the strange figure standing over us on the stage. "Seriously, Aoibheall, I really am done with people walking in on us. This is now beyond ridiculous."

"But *you* invoked *me*," says the woman. She's dressed smartly in a suit, but there's something so familiar about her. And if I thought that Aoibheall's eyes were green, well this woman's put them to shame.

"I invoked you?"

"It's Ériu," says Aoibheall. Her voice is flat, completely devoid of any character. It's odd and I don't like it.

Ériu. The Goddess of Ireland herself. "I'm naked and I'm post-orgasmic," I say, managing to go full librarian, despite my debauched state. "As lovely as it is to meet you, I really don't have time for it right now."

She crouches down beside me and tries to meet my eyes. I flinch away, curling my body until my face is pressed into Aoibheall's body. "No, thank you," I say.

"Do you know what I can offer?" she asks, astonishment in her voice. "The things I can give you, the power you could have?"

"No, *thank you*," I repeat, emphasising the thanking. I don't want a goddess of this calibre—of any calibre really—thinking that I'm ungrateful for their attentions. Don't fuck with the fae, but don't fuck with gods even more. Aoibheall starts to shuffle backward, and I growl and pull her closer. "Absolutely not, Aoibheall, you stay right where you are."

Ériu's laughter is unlike anything I've ever heard. In it I hear the waves crashing against the Cliffs of Moher, I hear creatures calling to each other in the Lough Navar forests, I hear people drinking and toasting each other all throughout the land. I hear everything that is Ireland.

"You're turning me down? For a mere fae queen?"

"Yes," I say sharply. "I'm sure you're very nice, but Aoibheall's mine, thank you very much." She's been saying all evening that I am hers, well it works both ways. Aoibheall clearly wasn't expecting me to say that though, because she looks stunned.

I peek across her shoulder and see Ériu nod in satisfaction. "You will do, Lizzie Byrne." And then she is gone.

"Do you think that will be the last unannounced visitor?" I ask Aoibheall, who still looks like she's been poleaxed. "Aoibheall?"

"You're claiming me as yours?" she asks. She is on her side and she is staring at me.

I take my hand and run it down her body, touching her for what actually might be the first time. So I take my time.

Light touches, feathering across her collarbones, down her shoulders to the tips of her fingers—which I have to stretch for, because mine aren't as long—and back up to flit over the swell of her breasts. Grazing one nipple and then the other, stroking down her stomach until I hit the top of her public bone.

I don't tease her the way she did me.

"Do you want me to touch you?"

"Yes," she whispers, almost reverently.

"Okay then." I stroke her clit, and then lower until my fingers are coated in her desire.

"Just there," she says, pressing my fingers back to her clit, and she kisses me as I stroke her, running my fingers over and around until she lifts her head and buries it in the crook of my neck.

Her breathing is coming faster, and I shrug my shoulder until she lifts her head slowly and looks at me. "You are mine," I tell her.

"I am yours," she says, and her legs shake and clamp together, and all I can feel is her clit throbbing against my fingers as she comes. "I am yours Lizzie. My mortal."

"Your mortal," I say. "Not even the Goddess of Éire could lure me away."

There's surprise in Aoibheall's eyes, and disbelief, and I kiss her firmly, trying to cement us, to reassure her that I'm not going anywhere.

Her arms come around me and she pulls me close. "I am yours," she says. And I see in her eyes that she believes me. "For as long as you'll have me, I am yours. I vow it."

Our lips meet, and she cups my face with such tenderness that I almost cry. "Thank you," I breathe. "For showing me all I could be."

"And thank you," she says. "For seeing it, and wanting me anyway."

The End

READ CLIODHNA'S BOOK

People have warned me away from the Golden Apple, that it's not a place for nice girls. But something draws me there anyway...to this club run by Dommes with magic at their fingertips.

Because I'm not as nice a girl as I seem. And when Cliodhna promises a night of exquisite pleasure, I'm ready to sign away my very soul in exchange.

Welcome to the Godstouched Universe, where the Gods interfere in the lives of mortals, magic leaks back into our world, and love conquers all.

Their Fruits like Honey is a sapphic Goblin Market retelling.

ALSO BY ALI WILLIAMS

Godstouched Universe

Forged in Flames: A Dragon Shifter Romance

Value in Visions: A Sapphic Psychic Romance

Married in Moonlight: A Sapphic Psychic Wedding

The Apples Hung like Stars: A Sapphic Fae Romance

Their Fruits like Honey: A Sapphic Fae Romance

Lure Me to the Deep: A Sapphic Mermaid Romance

Chase Me in the Woods: A Sapphic Shifter Romance

Catch Me in the Dark: A Sapphic Samhain Romance

Nix and Tell: A Sapphic Fae Romance

Never Nix Up: A Sapphic Fae Romance

Don't Give a Nix: A Sapphic Fae Romance

Erotic Romance

The Softest Kinksters Collection: An Erotic Romance Collection

Kink the Halls: A Sleeping with my Ex's Mum, Lesbian Christmas Romance

Flogging Faith: A Submissives of Rawhide Romance

Stuffie Hospital Books (as Ellie Rose)

A Little's Unicorn (Lillie and Aiden's book)

A Little's Reindeer (Georgie and Warren's book)

A Little's Lion (Kacie and Dex's book)

A Little's Patchwork Bear (Ralphie and Nate's book)

A Little's Witchy Bear (Rylie and Eve's book)

A Little's Engagement (Ralphie and Nate's sequel)

A Little's Monster (Christie and Dana's book)

A Little's Dino (Archie and Rebecca's book)

A Little's Elephant (Frankie and Grey's book)

A Little's Owl (Darcie and Richard's book)

A Little's Pegasus (Beanie and Abigail's book)

STUFFIE HOSPITAL LONDON BOOKS (AS ELLIE ROSE)

A London Little's Llama (Billie and Mark's book)

A London Little's Moo (Tillie and Alex's book)

A London Little's Dragon (Jamie and Marian's book)

A London Little's Giraffe (Mossie and Daniel's book)

A London Little's Penguin (Rubie and Anna's book)

A London Little's Pom Pom (Rosie and Eloise's book)

A London Little's Bunny (Essie and Ben's book)

A London Little's Octopus (Charlie and Leon's book)

A London Little's Tiger (Susie and Briana's book)

THE LITTLES' MARKET BY THE SEA BOOKS (AS ELLIE ROSE)

Isla (Isla and Rachel's book)

Emma (Emma and Bryn's book)

Liv (Liv and Cat's book)

Sage (Sage and Lily's book)

Tess (Tess and Willow's book)

Reba (Reba and Kirby's book)

Nicole (Nicole and Violet's book)

Brooke (Brooke and Jenny's book)

Morgan (Morgan and Rose's book)

Wyn (Wyn and Tel's book)

River (River and Alice's book)

Aubrey (Aubrey and Helen's book)

Skylar (Skylar and Gabrielle's book)

RAWHIDE RANCH BOOKS (AS ELLIE ROSE)

Mandi's Little Mother's Day (Mandi and Amelia's book)

ACKNOWLEDGMENTS

Lizzie and Aoibheall had me in a grip from the first moment that I considered their story. I've always loved Christina Rosetti's Goblin Market, and writing a story which features a glut of fruit sounded like so much fun. Of course, in this version of the story, the good girl lets loose, and revels in the abundance offered her. Lizzie doesn't abstain, she embraces.

This book is dedicated to Ash, with whom I working on a very exciting Godstouched Universe project. Their friendship and support, and willingness to nerd out with me over tarot at the drop of a hat is always appreciated.

I've also Zoomed with any number of people, but particularly EJ Frost, Rayanna Jamison, Aleksandr Voinov and LG Knight. Thanks for the company; it really helped!!

The writing community is myriad, and I am surrounded by more excellent authors than I could have ever hoped for. Their enthusiasm and encouragement are everything.

Teresa, of Wolfsparrow Covers, what can I say about these books but thank you? They are so beautiful, and capture exactly the vibes I wanted for these books.

And finally, to Abi, who walked me round the block when I had writer's block, who makes sure I'm fed and watered, and provides the best kind of inspiration. I adore you. Your patience with me and my special brand of being is more than I could have hoped for. I hope you feel as loved by me as I do by you.

And finally, dear reader, it is your turn. These books mean so much to me, so thank you for picking them up. This Godstouched Universe maybe be spicy—neurospicy as well as the other type—but it has heart. It has my heart. I hope you enjoy it.

ABOUT ALI

Ali Williams is a sapphic AuDHD author who writes intensely kinky paranormal romances as Ali, and fluffy and spicy age play romances as Ellie Rose.

Her PhD research focuses on the intersection between queerness and kink in feminist romance, and her sell-out online lecture series, Romancing the Discourse, discussed everything from how erotic romances use kink as liberation, to how paranormal romance can degender agency.

When she's not writing, she can invariably be found reading tarot, traipsing round the South Downs with her girlfriend, or playing boardgames with her queer, kinky, found family.